NEW MEXICO
TRIPTYCH

NEW MEXICO
TRIPTYCH

by
Fray Angélico Chávez
Illustrated by the Author

New Foreword
by
Marc Simmons

SANTA FE

Sunstone books may be purchased for educational, business, or sales promotional
use. For information please write: Special Markets Department, Sunstone Press,
P.O. Box 2321, Santa Fe, New Mexico 87504-2321.

Library of Congress Cataloging-in-Publication Data

Chavez, Angelico, 1910-1996.
  New Mexico triptych / by Fray Angélico Chávez ; illustrated by the author ; new
foreword by Marc Simmons.
     p. cm. -- (Southwest heritage series)
  Originally published: Paterson, N.J. : St. Anthony Guild Press, 1940.
  ISBN 978-0-86534-771-7 (pbk.: alk. paper)
  1. Southwestern States--Fiction. I. Title.
  PS3505.H625N49 2010
  813'.52--dc22

                    2010032185

WWW.SUNSTONEPRESS.COM
SUNSTONE PRESS / Post Office Box 2321 / Santa Fe, NM 87504-2321 /USA
(505) 988-4418 / orders only (800) 243-5644 / FAX (505) 988-1025

CONTENTS

I
THE SOUTHWEST HERITAGE SERIES

II
FOREWORD TO THIS EDITION
Marc Simmons

III
REVIEW
by
T. M. Pearce
The New Mexico Quarterly
August, 1940, Volume X, Number 3

IV
FACSIMILE OF 1940 EDITION

SOUTHWEST HERITAGE SERIES

I

THE SOUTHWEST HERITAGE SERIES

"The past is not dead. In fact, it's not even past."
—William Faulkner, *Requiem for a Nun*

The history of the United States is written in hundreds of regional histories and literary works. Those letters, essays, memoirs, biographies and even collections of fiction are often first-hand accounts by people who wanted to memorialize an event, a person or simply record for posterity the concerns and issues of the times. Many of these accounts have been lost, destroyed or overlooked. Some are in private or public collections but deemed to be in too fragile condition to permit handling by contemporary readers and researchers.

However, now with the application of twenty-first century technology, nineteenth and twentieth century material can be reprinted and made accessible to the general public. These early writings are the DNA of our history and culture and are essential to understanding the present in terms of the past.

The Southwest Heritage Series is a form of literary preservation. Heritage by definition implies legacy and these early works are our legacy from those who have gone before us. To properly present and preserve that legacy, no changes in style or contents have been made. The material reprinted stands on its own as it first appeared. The point of view is that of the author and the era in which he or she lived. We would not expect photographs of people from the past to be re-imaged with modern clothes, hair styles and backgrounds. We should not, therefore, expect their ideas and personal philosophies to reflect our modern concepts.

Remember, reading their words and sharing their thoughts is a passport back into understanding how the past was shaped and how it influenced today's world.

Our hope is that new access to these older books will provide readers with a challenging and exciting experience.

II

FOREWORD TO THIS EDITION
by
Marc Simmons

He has been called a renaissance man and New Mexico's foremost twentieth-century humanist by biographer Ellen McCracken. Any way you measure his career, Fray Angélico Chávez was an unexpected phenomenon in the wide and sunlit land of the American Southwest.

His life, which began at Wagon Mound, New Mexico in 1910, was filled with vigorous physical and intellectual activity. Above all, Fray Angélico was an independent and original thinker, traits not usually associated with someone in a religious order who takes a vow of humility.

In the decades following his ordination as a Franciscan priest in 1937, Chávez performed the difficult duties of an isolated backcountry pastor. His assignments included Hispanic villages and Indian pueblos. As an army chaplain in World War II, he accompanied troops in bloody landings on Pacific islands, claiming afterwards that because of his small stature, Japanese bullets always missed him.

In time despite heavy clerical duties, Fray Angélico managed to become an author of note, as well as something of an artist and muralist. Upon all of his endeavors, one finds, understandably, the imprint of his religious perspective. During nearly seventy years of writing, he published almost two dozen books. Among them were novels, essays, poetry, biographies, and histories. Sunstone Press is now bringing back into print some of the rare titles.

Upon his death in 1996, Chávez left his huge collection of documents and personal papers to Santa Fe's Palace of the Governor's History Library, one of the region's major research institutions. In that year, it was renamed the Fray Angélico Chávez Library and Photographic Archives.

Today, a handsome life-size statue of the *padre* in his Franciscan robe stands in front of the building on Washington Avenue. During the first severe winter after its unveiling, a good Samaritan placed a stocking cap on the head of the statue.

Throughout his life, Fray Angélico remained a confirmed Hispanophile. In the 1960s and 1970s, that stance won him the enmity of Chicano Activists, who rejected the Spanish side of their heritage. But Fray Angélico had spent too many years documenting the colonial record of New Mexicans' achievements on this far-flung frontier to succumb to the blandishments of anti-Spanish ideologues.

Indeed, of the many accolades he received in his lifetime, none pleased him more than the one bestowed upon him by Spain's King Juan Carlos: membership in the knightly Order of Isabel la Católica, granted in recognition of his contributions to learning and the arts.

All true aficionado's of the American Southwest's history and culture will profit by collecting and reading the significant body of work left to us by the remarkable Fray Angélico Chávez.

III

REVIEW
by
T. M. Pearce
The New Mexico Quarterly
August, 1940, Volume X, Number 3

Much has been said and written about regional literature in the Southwest. Yet most of the speakers and writers on the subject are individuals who were not born in the region, but have become conscious of its character by contrast with other places where they started out. They see the Southwest perhaps more clearly than people born here. Yet as creative writers they may not really know the psychology of people and place as does the native. As critics they may be tempted to prescribe what the Southwest should produce, given certain ingredients, skillful cooks, and proper recipes found in the annals of comparative literature.

I don't say one could have predicted Fray Chavez. No formula ever explains the genius for poetry or painting or story-telling, and Fray Chavez has a gift for all three. Yet one can explain and in part understand how the artistic tradition of Spanish New Mexico, the mysticism of Franciscan faith, and the folk-lore and fraternity of village life might, fortunately, join in a young man from Mora, New Mexico, educated at eastern schools of his Order, and stationed in a parish not far from the literary center of the Southwest.

During July [1940], Fray Angélico spoke at the University of New Mexico, reading his poetry and presenting his point of view as a poet. He said that it was love of words that seemed essentially poetry to him, and curiously love of words in English, not all of them English words, however. One has to mine through the words of harsh tone and flat significance for the store of sensuous and meaningful words accumulated from the Classic and Romance languages and almost every speech known to the globe. This artistry in words is not confined to Fray Angélico's poetry. His prose is apparently simple, effortless, flowing, but I suspect that before he writes a word and after, he sits reflectively choosing to leave or eliminate on the basis of specific quality in sound and color and fitness every mark on the page.

"Hunchback Madonna," the last of the three stories in *New Mexico Triptych*, is my favorite. Mana Seda, the central character, is a pious old woman so bent with age that as she creeps about in her black shawl people sometimes whisper, "She is like the Black Widow Spider." Injured in her youth, she was never considered among the maidens who became queens of the Virgin when her festival was held in May. For many years, Mana Seda has gathered the flowers for the garlands which the girls were to carry in this procession. She remembers, too, long, long ago when an image of the Virgin of Guadalupe intended for the church at El Tordo had been lost when the pack train from Chihuahua was attacked by Apaches.

A reviewer, however, must not tell an author's whole story. After seventy years of providing flowers for the festival, but never being chosen one of the flower maids, Mana Seda finally gets the reward for her piety. And in the meantime a santero has painted the Virgin on her shawl. "And so Mana Seda led all the queens that evening, slowly and smoothly, not like a black widow now, folks observed, but like one of those little white moths moving over alfalfa fields in the moonlight."

There are two other stories: "The Penitente Thief," with more of humor and yet the same pathos; "The Angel's New Wings," beautiful and moving. The illustrations have been done by the author, pen and ink sketches, harmonious in line and careful in detail. Fine literature and good reading lie in *New Mexico Triptych*.

IV

FACSIMILE OF 1940 EDITION

NEW MEXICO
TRIPTYCH

▼▼▼

FRAY ANGELICO CHAVEZ

NEW MEXICO TRIPTYCH

Being three panels and three accounts:
1. The Angel's New Wings; 2. The Penitente
Thief; 3. Hunchback Madonna

Illustrated by the Author

Nihil obstat: FR. HYACINTHUS BLOCKER, O. F. M., Cen. dep. —
Imprimi potest: FR. ADALBERTUS ROLFES, O. F. M., Min. Prov.,
Cincinnati, 3. 2. 40. — *Nihil obstat:* HENRY J. ZOLZER, Cen. lib. —
Imprimatur: †THOMAS H. MCLAUGHLIN, Ep. Patersonensis, 3. 30. 40.

To

"Coronado's Children"

My People

Contents

▼▼▼

I

THE ANGEL'S NEW WINGS

▼▼▼

THE ANGEL'S NEW WINGS

HISKERY old Nabor blew over his flossy chin into the two holes he had finished gouging in the shoulders of a small wooden figure. Into one he stuck a newly whittled wing. It fitted loosely, but that could be fixed later with a sliver or two. He picked the other wing from his lap, pushed it into the second socket, and then stared into his empty hands!

No amount of painful peering under chair and table and bed disclosed the missing angel. The little fireplace of baked adobe in the corner held its single black pine-knot simmering on a heap of scarlet coals. The angel had simply vanished, slipped out of his hand the way sparrows or trout usually do, only much more swiftly.

3

From days unremembered Nabor Roybal had enjoyed the right of setting up the *nacimiento* in the old adobe church every time Christmas came to Rio Dormido. Not one living soul in Rio Dormido could recall when he as a youth had carved each figure out of pine. There was a smiling little Infant with a slim Mary to kneel at its side, and a Joseph who leaned drowsily on his staff; there were over a dozen shepherds in varied, stiff poses, and an unnumbered herd of sheep — folks said he added a sheep every year. An ox and an ass were the most true to life, everybody thought. And above all these hung an angel with outspread, stubby wings.

After the corn was brought in and husked, and the wheat or beans threshed by tiny black hoofs in the goat-corral, Nabor started to look forward to his beloved task. The first snow flurries creeping over the mesas surrounding the village told him that the great day drew nearer; and when the Padre wore deep penitential purple for Mass in the small but massive mud church of the Twelve Apostles, Nabor knew for sure that the Kingdom of God was at hand. Then it was high time to open his ancient carved chest of dovetailed boards where slept his *santos* in a welter of numberless wooden sheep.

But this year the harvest hustling, followed by a too early cold wave over the mesas, and also the final straws of old age, had forced Nabor to keep to his little room, its snug white-washed comfort spoiled only by the inseparable aches in the old fellow's limbs and lungs. He could scarcely drag himself to the church the first Sunday the Padre put on purple. Christmas Eve found him unable to move from his little fireplace. Saddest of all, other hands were to set up the crib, for the first time since the little figures had been carved.

That afternoon Padre Arsenio sent some boys over to Nabor's house for the old chest with its quaint images. From that moment the traditions of generations began to be broken in various ways; for the priest had come back shortly afterward with one of the statues. There was a half-amused, half-pitying look on the young Padre's lean, dark face.

"Nabor, you must fix the angel for tonight," he had said. "The girl who was dusting the figures caught the wings with her rag and —"

The old man took the damaged seraph and squinted at it from odd angles before speaking. "I always thought the wings were too short anyway. My little Padre, soon I shall carve new ones, bigger and lighter ones."

"And one of the boys broke the burro's left fore-hoof," Padre Arsenio added, stepping astride the threshold. "But that can be hidden by the straw."

Shaking his white, shaggy head Nabor had opened his knife, reached for a piece of firewood and begun whittling. His mind limped back right away to the more even ground of the past, the time when he had shaped these little figures. Before that, as a boy, he had helped his father carve the corbels under the church rafters, and the twisted columns flanking the high reredos. Those days breathed reverence and faith. He recalled how both young and old kept a watch in the church on Christmas Eve before the midnight Mass, his father leading the singing of old Spanish carols. Those ancient traditions were slowly being broken — and now his dear little statues, too. Nabor thought all this aloud as he cut and blew, blew and whittled and scraped on bigger, better wings for the herald angel.

It was already dark when the Padre returned. This time his lean young face was far from amused. "Nabor," he panted, "all the images have been stolen!"

Nabor did not appear shocked by the news. He always looked stunned. After a silent span he asked with seeming calmness, "Who would want to steal them after all these years?"

"There are people in Santa Fé or Taos who buy them for good money, Nabor. Some good-for-nothing in Rio Dormido has run away with them for that purpose."

Nabor did not say anything more, did not even hear what the priest said after that. The Padre left him sitting on his chair by the fire, the two finished wings on his lap, and in one hand the little angel with two holes dug in its shoulders.

Slowly, Nabor put in one wing, then the other — and the angel vanished.

▼▼▼

A straight icy draught slicing the room's warmth made Nabor turn to the only window. On one of the four misty panes was a dark blotch, like the uneven outline of an angel flying. Nabor stuck his trembling hand through the dark spot, for the glass had been neatly cut out, or burned, or melted away. A few yards away from the window ran a fence of upright cedar posts, set close together like organ-pipes. Between two of these knotty palings was an opening of like shape. Brought into line, the hole in the window-light and the hole in the fence pointed like gunsights to the brightly lit front of the town dancehall.

The old man lost no time in looking for his coat and hat. The smart air outside gripped and shook his palsied frame, but not his purpose. Reeling and bobbing as though he had springs in his neck and under each shapeless shoe, Nabor reached the crowded *portal* of the dancehall.

Unnoticed by the men, who were intently watching two rolling, cursing brawlers on the porch floor, he touched a young fellow's elbow. "Boy," he stammered, "have you seen the angel? He flew straight this way." Had he been asked something more earthy, the youth might have returned his attention to the wrestlers. Instead he stared at Nabor.

"It was the angel of the crib," the old man explained further. "It had new wings, longer than the old ones."

The young man grinned wisely and gestured with a shrug. "Oh, yes, yes; it knocked off my sombrero when it flew into the hall."

Nabor thanked him and went in the doorway, only to be snatched into the swirl of crowded dancers, everybody ignoring him, pushing him and spinning him around from one couple to another. He was in the middle of the long room when the guitars and fiddles stopped, and someone called his name.

"Nabor, are you looking for a partner?"

"No, I am looking for an angel."

"That would be a wonderful partner for a polka or *la raspa,* old man. What sort of an angel is she?"

"It is the angel of the crib, and his wings are newer than the old ones."

By this time many of the revelers had gathered around him. "Ah!" rang the voice of a laughing girl. "His wings are newer than the old ones! There he goes — up there!"

All eyes looked up with Nabor's at the rough rafters where a frightened sparrow flitted from one end of the hall to the other. The music started anew, and the dancers fell to milling around merrily. Once more Nabor was jostled about, until he staggered out of the hall's rear doorway. From across the deep-rutted lane, the brightly lighted windows of the village store shone into his face. A familiar dark outline on the large door pane drew him stumbling over the frost-hardened wheel-tracks.

The dark shape on the door-light turned out to be an eagle, pasted on the glass to advertise some brand of canned food. Inside, Nabor found himself in a maze of streamers trimmed with tinsel. A little Santa Claus, with a cotton beard whiter and longer than his own, seemed to greet him merrily. The fat store-keeper, who was weighing out some sugar with the added pressure of his thumb, called out to ask whether Nabor wanted something in a hurry.

"Did you see an angel fly through here? It was the angel of the crib, and he flew off when I put those new and larger wings on him."

The man behind the scales chuckled as he pulled out a silver dollar. "Friend Nabor, this is the only thing with wings that flies in here, and it flies out much faster."

Nabor shook his whiskers and shuffled outside in time to hear the whistling whirr of strong wings aloft somewhere behind the store. Supporting himself along the crooked adobe wall, he turned the rear corner and all but bumped into the dark shape of a man carrying a sack out of the storekeeper's corn-crib. The prowler was about to drop his burden when he recognized the harmless intruder.

"Excuse me, *señor*," said the old man. "I just heard the angel fly behind this house. Did you see him?"

Before slipping away into the shadows, the man pointed mutely up at the dark sky. The silver shape of a startled pigeon wheeled about, like one of those tin lids that boys spin into the air, and came sailing back to the granary.

Nabor would have turned his steps homeward had not his eye caught the same bewitching outline on the goat-corral across the arroyo. Plainly stamped on the door of a shed on one side of the corral was the shape of wings and body, even a halo about the head. But the halo turned out to be only a knot-hole, and the rest a weather-mark on the rough planks.

Nevertheless, Nabor opened the door, which was slightly ajar, and went into the shed. The sharp, heaty scent of goats stung his nostrils as he paused to make sure if he had heard voices. A whisper, distinct in the smelly darkness, came to his ears. "Who can it be?" said a woman's voice; it was the store-keeper's wife, whom Nabor recognized.

"You people in there," he spoke softly, "have you seen an angel?"

A strange silence followed his query until Nabor explained: "It was the angel of the crib. When I fitted him with clean new wings he flew out of my hands."

"Yes, over there on the corner post," whispered the man, whose companion began to giggle. Nabor turned around to see a rooster which had flown up on a post and was cocking a curious head their way.

The goat-corral was the last structure on this side of Rio Dormido, and Nabor would have turned back had he not seen a silver flash on a large yellow pine that had long managed to thrive at the foot of the mesa not far away. Cries like those of a baby floated faintly down from the black needle-clusters. He was sure now that it was the angel — it moved up, down, up, against the lower part of the trunk. As he neared the tree a flock of frightened piñon jays flew away with babylike whimperings. But the angel still clung to the trunk, the way he used to hang upon the crib in the church. For Nabor, stumbling ever closer, the quest was ended.

Suddenly the thing stirred, tore itself backward from the rough bark, and flew with a soft, clapping noise to the mesa in measured downward swoops and upward jerks, like the flight of a flicker or any other kind of woodpecker. But that, too, would naturally be the flight of anything with wings of wood. Besides, did not his ears catch that wooden clapping? The thought put new strength in Nabor's legs as he began to climb toward the bleak rim of the mesa sharply lined against a hazily moonlit sky.

It was not moonlight, however, that lit the higher terrain, Nabor soon found out. As his head rose above the low palisade of tufa boulders, he stood frozen in his tracks to see a little figure hovering a few feet above the tableland. It was bathed in an unearthly glow. Its body was the same age-worn figure in faded colors which he had so often caressed with rough but loving fingers. Its wings were fresh, unpainted firewood, and they moved a little, like those of a soaring hawk, for Nabor had not had time to fasten them tightly with tiny pegs. He could even hear them squeak in their sockets.

And there were shepherds watching, his own little wooden shepherds in stiff poses, with surprised faces, *and keeping the night watches over their flocks* — his own little sheep that sprawled half-hidden all over the dried prairie grass.

And the angel said to them: "Fear not, for this day is born to you a Saviour, Who is Christ the Lord, in the city of David. And this shall be a sign to you. You shall find the Infant wrapped in swaddling clothes, and laid in a manger."

And suddenly there was with the angel a multitude of the heavenly army, beings of the same size as the angel but not of wood, *praising God and saying: "Glory to God in the highest, and on earth peace to men of good will."*

With this the sprite-like chorus vanished, and the angel of the crib swept down to the village of adobe with the jerky swoops of a flicker, while the aroused shepherds began to round up their flocks and drive them down the edge of the mesa.

▼▼▼

Nabor hurried back to Rio Dormido, past the silent pine and goat-corral, past the now darkened store and dancehall, and into the dimly lit church of the Twelve Apostles. The Padre was already intoning the *Gloria* at the candle-banked altar. Nabor strode shakily between the rows of worshipers, unaware of the knowing glances and smiles which they exchanged among themselves, for his rheumy gaze was fixed on the empty crib far in front near the altar. A flutter of wings among the carved *vigas* and corbels above made everybody look up. The people saw a bewildered sparrow. But Nabor saw a little angel of wood which sailed down to the crib and with a soft click and a clump hooked himself at his wonted place above the crib.

As the old man knelt down, the rear wall of the crib shook somewhat, and through the open gate shuffled an ox over the straw. The animal doubled its forelegs, rolled over on its side, and regarded Nabor with swaying jaws. Then came an old man with a staff leading a limping burro on which rode a pretty maiden. Nabor felt sorry for the donkey, which winced each time its hoofless stump touched the ground. Tenderly Joseph lifted the kneeling woman from the donkey's back; gently he laid her on a pile of straw; and there she lay in quiet, as though she were wholly spent from a long journey, her knees drawn up as she had been carved long ago.

By and by Padre Arsenio sang the *Credo,* and when the choir came to the words, *"Et incarnatus est de Spiritu Sancto ex Maria Virgine,"* the people in the nave knelt down with much noise. Right away Mary woke and raised herself in her kneeling posture on the straw. Now Nabor noticed with wonder that the statue, whose slim waist he had carved with delicate touch while turning tender *Aves* on his tongue, was seemingly great. And whilst his eye wondered, his ear caught a low noise, like the scraping of a knife on a stick. It was Joseph, leaning on his staff, and snoring softly.

The bell of Consecration woke neither Mary from her rapture nor Joseph from his slumber. For a brief spell, when the priest raised aloft the Host, and then the Chalice, Nabor had turned to the altar. As he peered back into the crib he found Mary, now maidenly slim as he had carved her, kneeling beside the manger. Joseph, too, stood staring down over his staff at the little wooden Child that smiled at them from the straw. And immediately the rear wall began to quake as droves of sheep rushed in, as sheep will do, crushing each other in a shouldering pack. They sprawled all about, some even crawling under the manger, as the panting shepherds followed after with expressions of awe and joy.

Later, the bell at the altar tinkled again. Nabor left the crib for the first time with anxious backward glances, and stumbled to the Communion railing, where men, women and children were elbowing each other for a place. Nabor could not hold himself in the meantime from looking back at the nave. At a glance he saw the woman of the goat-corral, drowsily swinging her rosary beads from her fingers; besides her sat her sleepy-eyed husband, the fat storekeeper. Behind her were the women and girls who had pushed him around the dancehall floor; of their male companions, some leaned lazily against the walls, others stood idly about the blazing stove.

When Nabor returned and knelt once again before the *nacimiento,* he noticed to his dismay that the shepherds with their flocks were already gone. He had no time to wonder before he heard a faint click. The angel had unhooked itself and had dropped lightly at Joseph's side, whispering something into his ear. Nabor drew closer. *"Arise,"* said the angel, *"and take the Child and His mother, and fly into Egypt; and be there until I shall tell thee. For it will come to pass that Herod will seek the Child to destroy Him."* Thus saying, the angel flitted back to his hook.

Mary grasped the Child to her breast, and Joseph lifted them both onto the burro's back. Joseph led it out limping under its sweet swaying burden, leaving the gate open behind them. Nabor knelt there overcome by the rise of dismay in his breast, gazing reproachfully at the ox, which glared back at him chewing its cud. At last the beast rolled back to its knees, stood up with an effort, and it too went out with slow, shuffling gait.

▼▼▼

The people were all gone when Padre Arsenio came back from the sacristy wrapped in his woolen cloak. He did not see the trembling old man crouched at the crib until he had returned from barring the front doors with a heavy beam and from snuffing out the paraffin candles in their tin sconces along the walls.

"So you had to come to the midnight Mass, Nabor?" the Padre spoke, raising him up from the cold floor. "We missed the adoration of the Child this year. I am very sorry the images were stolen."

Nabor's eyes regarded the Padre's with bewilderment. Perhaps the young cleric was somewhat touched in the head, like the rest of the world. The thought in Father Arsenio's mind was that Nabor was at the end of his days, mentally as well as bodily. Sharing part of his mantle with the stooped, ragged shoulders, he led the old man to his rooms for a sip of hot coffee or wine. As he blew out the last candles by the side door, darkness swallowed up the corbels, the reredos, the empty crib and the lonely angel with its new wings.

II

THE PENITENTE THIEF

▼▼▼

THE PENITENTE THIEF

I

"... there were two evildoers led with Him."

HE sad, meaningful days of Holy Week came to San Ramon as usual. On Palm Sunday evening the *penitentes* gathered in the town *cantina,* as their forefathers had done, to go the rounds at the bar for the last time until Holy Saturday. The days between would be taken up with long fasts and watches within the thick-walled *morada* up on the mountain slope. There would be midnight processions of scourging and cross-bearing among the scrub-oaks and cedars and, for a fit ending, the yearly crucifixion on Good Friday noon.

After looking over the line of shaggy heads across the counter, the *cantinero* turned to their leader. "The brotherhood is falling fast, no? Not half so many as other years."

25

The *hermano mayor* replied with a slow shrug. "*Si,* one-half they leave us when the Archbishop sends letters from Santa Fé."

Shaking his head in sympathy, the saloonkeeper refilled a score of glasses. "*Amigos,* this is on the house. To the faithful twenty — *salud!*"

"Twenty?" said the *hermano mayor.* "Twenty-two, counting Lucero and Maldonado over there!"

But Lucero and Maldonado were not bothering about numbers. Filling out his ample black suit to the last stitch, Maldonado sat very stiffly at a gambling table, his wide-brimmed beaver ready to drop from his ear, his under chin rolling limp over a silk string-necktie. Across from him and a drained quart bottle peered Lucero's mummy face, swathed in the ragged collar of his sheepskin and a woolen cap of uncertain hue. The two were beyond waking, the brethren well knew, and so they tramped away to their mountain retreat without them; while the *cantinero,* with the indifference of long practice, dragged them to a small rear room where he cached them among smelly heaps of horse blankets.

It was a strange thing, the friendship of these two. Maldonado was the town *politico,* very sly and canny as a lawyer, and a fairly successful gambler. Lucero was — just poor Lucero. Their common bond lay in the *hermandad,* which called their attention only when Holy Week came around or when a brother died, and in their drinking spells, which brought them to the nest of horse blankets quite often. Each spree lasted thirty-six hours at the least, very often forty-eight, every single one a span of utter forgetfulness, except for short but very lively dreams just before waking.

Maldonado always dreamed about snakes and the like. Rattlers as thick as logs slithered after him, or scorpions bigger than steers, with red tails poised in the air, chased him over endless plateaus. Lucero's dreams were of a calmer nature, always the same but for the ending; that differed each time. He saw himself as a puny lad living with an old, old aunt in that small *jacal* of cedar and adobe by the arroyo. He saw himself living there alone in his teens, as a youth, and as a man. But at every stage he found himself taking things, such as foodstuffs from the store, money and jewels from ladies' rooms, chickens from farmyards, fruit and green maize from orchards and *milpas*. An outstanding event was the Governor's visit to San Ramon. Governor Wallace, who had just written a novel about the Christ, was shaking hands with the ranchers and townsfolk. While holding Lucero's hand, he turned to an aide and remarked that this fellow made a fine model for the Good Thief. It was only later that His Excellency found his gold watch and chain missing.

His best venture, however, was the theft of a rare Navajo *bayeta* blanket from Doña Luisa's porch. It was the size that chiefly drew his eyes to it, and he took it to Santa Fé with the hope of getting some fifteen *pesos*. He got fifty dollars from an *Americano* who, mentally of course, valued it at a much higher price.

Lately the town merchant, Don Jacobo Rosenberg, had opened a bank for the benefit of the wealthy ranchers in the county. Lucero was beginning to devise a plan for robbing this bank, when he felt himself rudely shaken and heard a familiar voice in the dark.

"Eh, Maldonado?" he mumbled. "For why do you cut me my dream?"

"*Ay de mi,* Lucero," came the reply in the close gloom. "Would that you had cut mine. It was tarantulas this time, black and hairy, bigger than bison, herds of them chasing me!"

"But, my dear friend, I was just finding a good way of robbing the bank of Don Jacobo —"

"God forbid, Lucero! I have two thousand *pesos* in it. Besides, the government will catch you sure and lock you up in its *calabozo* for twenty years. Listen to me, *amigo mio.* Steal from people, cheat at cards or rob widows, even play dirty politics — but never rob the bank or steal a horse. The government or the vigilantes will get you!"

The sound of their voices brought the saloonkeeper to the door, and the two sat up, shielding their bleary eyes against the lamplight from the barroom.

"Very poor *penitentes* you make," he said jovially. "Here you are sleeping the hours away while the brothers up there take the discipline."

With a start Maldonado rolled to his feet. "Have they already left? *Señor,* how long have they been gone?"

The *cantinero* counted his fingers. "Oh, I would say about four days, four days to the very hour. My friends, this is Thursday evening!"

The startled pair were for hurrying off right away, but on being offered a bite to eat, they realized that they were very hungry and very weak. When they had done gorging themselves with jerked meat, *chile* and *tortillas,* both arose full of zest and eager to join their brethren. Maldonado bought a pint of whiskey "for strength on the journey." Out on the cold street they met groups of *terciarios* and other fraternities, some of whom were former *penitentes,* on their way to the Mission where a night-long wake was being kept before the Repository. Soon the two friends were out on the steep road leading to the *morada,* and long before it came in sight, the flask had been emptied and flung away.

The *penitentes'* stronghold showed no signs of life, as the only opening in the yard-thick walls was the single, heavily guarded door. All the windows faced a small patio in the center. Arriving at the door, Maldonado asked his companion for the secret signal.

"You hit the door twice with the foot and you say: *'Two evildoers were led with Him!'* "

"Meaning me and you," Maldonado chuckled. Then he stiffened and grabbed Lucero by his sheepskin collar. "Do you hear it? The *pito!*"

Lucero heard it, too, the weird wail of the *penitentes'* flute somewhere on the mountainside. They were late for the Thursday night procession! Each snatched a yucca scourge from the

doorpost, seemingly hung there for them, and took the path
leading to the Calvario, throwing off their clothes piecemeal
and stumbling over the rocks as fast as their numbed feet could
carry them. At the first turn they saw a light bobbing among the
pines, signaling them to hurry. Quickening their pace they soon
caught up with the procession, the sight of which filled them
with no small wonder.

For there were only three *penitentes* here, none of whom
they had seen before. The flute-player and the one with the lantern were comely youths in very neat overalls. The cross-bearer
between them wore a long white gown, and the usual black
mask covered his head entirely. The strangers acted as though
they had been expecting them, and the two friends, moved by
some unknown power, silently fell in line behind them, their
whips singing in the crisp air as they cracked in unison over
their bare backs. Whenever the cross-carrier fell they laid their
scourges on him, according to their ritual, until he arose with
the aid of his companions and trudged on till the next fall.

Lucero noticed particularly how much he bled. Shards of slag on the path shimmered crimson whenever the light of the lantern fell on his tracks. Most of the time the light was held in front of him so that he could pick out beds of flint chips or crawling cactus, in order purposely to step on them. Once, where the trail led over a smooth granite surface, the streamlets of blood left a design which reminded Lucero, he knew not why, of that Navajo blanket he had stolen from Doña Luisa. At last they came to a small cairn topped by a cross, a *descanso,* or resting-place for the weary cross-bearer. While the young men removed the heavy *madero* from his shoulder, Maldonado and Lucero sat down on the pile of stones, feeling very tired, very sleepy, as though they could sleep through four more days, maybe five. . . .

And there the brotherhood found them, almost frozen to death, when they came in procession at midnight. Back in the *morada,* they were stripped, laid on tables, and bathed with whiskey inside and out until, toward morning, they opened be-

wildered eyes. No one believed their story. They were drunk
and were seeing things, said every one of the brethren. Maldonado himself believed it was all a nightmare, like the scorpions and the tarantulas. But Lucero was not so sure.

▼▼▼

II

". . . one on the right . . . the other on the left."

THE following year Holy Week came early, but not so early for Lucero, who spent most of the time in jail. At the end of one of his sprees behind the *cantina* he had hatched out a plot for robbing the Mission of San Ramon. There was in the ancient adobe church a large chalice which had come with the first settlers and which was used only on big feasts. It was solid gold, not merely gold-plated, and of *oro mexicano,* having very little alloy. Rubies and garnets studded the foot and knob and the underside of the cup.

On a spring midnight Lucero broke into the sacristy and made away with this, San Ramon's chief treasure. But he had not reckoned with the Padre's piety. Unknown to his flock, the old priest used to spend the entire night on his knees before the altar, and he easily recognized the prowler's jagged silhouette

against the sacristy window. He quietly went to the sheriff's
house across the street, and poor Lucero was caught red-handed
before he even reached his adobe and cedar *jacal* by the arroyo.

It took all of Maldonado's legal knowledge and political
pull to get him out of jail at the end of ten months. Maldonado
was very kind about it all. "It was not your fault, Lucero," he
had said. "Who would have thought that such an old man
spent the night in the church? In the future be more careful.
Like myself. Take for an example old Doña Encarnación Lopez.
She is supposed to be getting a fat pension from Washington
because her husband years ago helped defeat the Confederates
at Glorieta. But I am her *abogado;* I get more from it than she
does, and no one knows the difference."

"*Ay, amigo,*" Lucero had answered. "But never let Toribio
Lopez, that crazy nephew of hers, find it out. He strikes like the
vibora as soon as you step on its rattles."

"He is too ignorant to find out, Lucero. As I always say to
you, cheat the widow and the orphan, even kill — but do not

rob the bank or steal a horse. The government or the vigilantes will surely get you!"

When the *penitentes* rallied at the saloon on Palm Sunday evening, both Lucero and Maldonado were there in mind as well as in body. The *hermano mayor* had seen to it that they stayed sober, for two of the older members had died during the winter and he wanted all the remaining twenty to take part. Even now the two were not allowed more than a small glassful apiece. Once at the *morada,* however, they entered wholeheartedly into the spirit of the brotherhood, hoping to atone the better for their sins the more they crisscrossed their backs with scarlet welts.

Every night there was a penitential procession to the Calvario, and then it was that memories of last year throbbed through Lucero's brain. But he said nothing. He said nothing until Maundy Thursday evening, when one of the men recalled the incident and everybody laughed. Jumping to his feet, Lucero swore warmly by San Ramon and all the blessed saints that it was not a drunkard's dream.

The brethren had seldom seen Lucero angry before. Calling
for silence, the *hermano mayor* said to him: "Brother, you have
a right to your belief, and so have we to ours. This is Holy
Thursday. You and Maldonado are not drunk now, so both of
you will go out and see if you can find them."

Maldonado was as loath to go as Lucero was eager, but the
earnest begging of the whole *hermandad* at length prevailed.
As they were about to leave, the leader asked them if they re-
membered this year's countersign for use on their return.

"*Si, señor*," Lucero replied. "Kick each doorpost once and
say: '*One on the right, the other on the left!*'"

It had been snowing since noon, and the two friends found
themselves walking in a dark and eerie silence that made their
footfalls sound as though horses were feeding at their heels.
But there was not the faintest hoot of a *pito* nor the least flicker
of a light, even when they came to the first turn in the path.
Maldonado was for returning at once, but his partner begged
him to go as far as the *descanso*.

Suddenly Lucero's heart leaped up, for there by the resting-place, on the very spot where they had left them the year before, stood the three strangers, as if waiting for the two friends to resume the journey. Taking the whips which one of the youths handed to them, they stripped to the waist and fell in line, slowly striking their backs right and left as the *pitero* went playing his flute and his twin swung his lantern before the cross-bearer. When the latter fell, they scourged him; when he arose they brought the disciplines back over their own shoulders and silently followed after. Lucero's eyes were charmed by the amber glow of the lantern which turned patches of snow into gleaming gold, into rich *oro mexicano;* and the blood-stains on the snow sparkled in spots like cut rubies, in others like dark, polished garnets. Somehow, it made him think of the chalice of San Ramon.

At last they reached the Calvario, a flat shelf of ground against a bare side of the mountain. The cross was placed on the snow with its foot next to a deep hole, and the man in white laid himself upon it. While the young men bound his arms, Lucero and Maldonado tied his legs to the beam with thongs which one of the youths had tossed over. It seemed to Lucero that there were holes in the man's feet, but he could not be sure, so encrusted were they with clotted blood and even prickly bits of cactus. Again as if out of nowhere, the youths produced a pair of long leather lariats by which they pulled the cross upright, the two friends holding its foot to the deep snowy socket, into which it sank and was made fast with stones.

All this was done in silence. For a while they stood there, Lucero on the victim's right, Maldonado on his left; and it seemed to the former that those eyes behind that black mask were fixed on himself. At length, at some unspoken sign from the youths which they somehow understood, the two friends started to walk away and were soon running with all their might back to the *morada.*

The brethren were staggered at first at the sight of the two gory, panting figures, but not for long. While both were trying to tell in one voice what had happened to them, a member cried out: "It is all made up! They have whipped themselves to blood and run themselves out of breath to save their faces!" The cry spread like a flame, but was quenched at once by a gesture from their leader.

"*Hermanos,*" he addressed them. "Give these men a chance to speak. You, Maldonado, are a man of learning and good sense. Can you prove to us what you are saying, as you would to a jury?"

"*Sí, señor.* You can all go over and see for yourselves, for we have crucified him!"

Again there was a stir, and again the leader raised his hand. "Brothers, we will all go in procession now instead of at midnight. Leave your disciplines behind; put on your hats and coats and bring your pistols and rifles. This might be a trick of Tom Hutchins and his ranch hands, who do not love our people overmuch. *Vamos!*"

Deep misgivings began to well in the breasts of the two friends when they scanned the path at the *descanso* and found no other footprints than their own. So it was all the way to the Calvario — not a trace of the three strangers, not even the deep furrow plowed by the dragging timber of the cross. When the Calvario itself hove into view, there stood the tall cross, stark against the white flank of the mountain; but the youths were gone, and also the man in the white gown. In fact, there were no other footmarks on the whole clearing except those of Lucero and Maldonado. And the cross was none other than the brotherhood's own *madero*.

That there was something here beyond the natural nobody dared to deny. Two men could not have carried that weighty pine trunk all the way from the *morada* without leaving telltale marks in the snow. Much less could they have raised it unaided, and without ruffling the white carpet roundabout. There was only one explanation, and the word was swiftly passed around until it reached the ears of the two bewildered friends: *"Embru-jados* — bewitched!" Someone had laid the evil eye on these two.

If Lucero agreed, he said nothing. Maldonado, however, really believed that he was hexed and begged his fellows to keep it all a secret, according to the rules. On their return to headquarters, all sat around and idly waited for Holy Saturday; even the Good Friday crucifixion was abandoned because no one volunteered to have himself tied to the *madero,* as had been done in other years from time immemorial.

They straggled into the village on Saturday morning just as the mission bells rang out the glad tidings of the risen Lord. Some of them sought the shelter of the saloon, where Maldonado bought a quart of *aguardiente* to wash away, so he whispered into Lucero's ear, the evil spell that had been laid upon them.

▼▼▼

III

"Lord, remember me. . . ."

WHEN Holy Week came to San Ramon again, there was the traditional gathering in the saloon on Palm Sunday night. But Maldonado and Lucero were not to be seen at the bar or at the gambling table, nor were they among the horse blankets. The *penitentes* said it was too bad, and the *cantinero* regretfully shook his head as he set up their glasses anew.

For several days Lucero had lain in his hut suffering from sharp pains in his stomach. Months before it had begun to rebel against the least drop of liquor, and of late it protested even at the touch of food, so that weakness added to pain had forced the poor fellow to his cot.

Had Doña Luisa not learned of his plight in time, he would have slowly starved to death, for during these days Maldonado happened to be on a solitary spree in his own house. Indeed,

Lucero had seen little of his old crony since he was obliged to stop drinking. When Doña Luisa first stepped into the *jacal* one morning, the sick man thought she came to see him about that Navajo blanket. But she did not suspect him at all. So kind and tender was she, so motherly even, that when she offered to bring the doctor at her own expense, he had to own the theft. The good lady melted into tears and forgave him altogether, saying she would not tell a soul. The doctor came later on and gave him some medicines which lessened the pain. He also prescribed milk and thin, unleavened cakes, not *tortillas* by any means, as his sole diet, and Doña Luisa took it upon herself to furnish all these things.

The only visitor was the *hermano mayor,* who had stopped in on Palm Sunday noon to see if he was going with the brethren. "I wish very much to go," Lucero had told him, "but my legs will not hold me up. Tell the brothers to pray for me. If I get better by Thursday I will go. I want to be there on Thursday. *Señor,* what is the secret password for this year?"

"Knock three times and say: *'Lord, remember me.'*"

The days following were lonely ones, except for the calls made by the doctor or Doña Luisa. Maundy Thursday, however, brought several very significant visitors. The first to call was Maldonado, early in the morning. "Lucero, my dear friend," he said, looking haggard and scared, "I just woke up and they told me you are very sick. You look pale."

"*Ay, amigo mio,*" Lucero answered. "The doctor said yesterday I will not live long. Pretty soon comes the last long sleep, and without your company, Maldonado. No waking from it, and no dreams."

"But are you not afraid to die, Lucero, to be buried among all those dead people in the *campo santo?* Listen to me, Lucero. I had the worst dream this morning, not rattlesnakes or centipedes this time, but a ghost. It was old Doña Encarnación Lopez. She twisted my toes until I woke up yelling with pain!"

Lucero smiled wanly. "It was only a whiskey dream, like the tarantulas. The old lady cannot hurt you for cheating her of her pension. She is dead three months already. She died on New Year's."

"Ay, Lucero, but you do not know the truth. I must tell you that she did not die — I killed her. She grew suspicious and I stopped her breath —"

The approaching footsteps of the next callers stopped short Maldonado's confession. Doña Luisa appeared smiling at the door, followed by the stooped figure of the parish priest. Both looked at Maldonado and passed the time of day; then the lady turned to her patient:

"I have brought you another doctor, my son. You know what the *medico* said yesterday. So you will let the Padre prepare you, no?"

Lucero regarded the priest for a while. "What Doña Luisa says must be right. *Señor cura,* it is well."

Doña Luisa grasped the other man's sleeve as he tried to slip away. "Lucero, you ought to ask your friend here to have a word with the Padre, too!"

Maldonado grinned sheepishly. "But I am not dying," he stammered, and stumbled out of the house.

The next visitors did not arrive until late in the evening. Lucero lay awake in the dark wishing that he could be at the *morada,* or rather, on the rocky trail that led to the Calvario. He chided himself for not going, as the night air was unusually warm, even though there was snow all over the ground. Suddenly, a burning pain coursed through his middle and he cried aloud, "Lord, remember me!"

There was a pause after the echo of his cry had died down. Then it was that he heard three distinct knocks at the door. Thinking it was Maldonado, he bade him enter. His heart gave a jerk and seemed to stop when the door opened and let in the light of a lantern. There stood the two handsome youths of whom he had been thinking all day long, and in the amber glow beyond them was the Penitente in White with his heavy cross. He wore no mask now. His Face was the most beautiful thing Lucero had ever seen, sad and pale though it appeared beneath a thick wreath of thorns. It made him forget his pain. It made him feel strong again. Quickly he put on his shoes and clothes, his old sheepskin, his woolen cap, and once more the strange procession of last year and the year before went on its way over the snows.

Instead of heading for the *morada,* they took the arroyo bed toward the Hutchins' ranch, whose corrals skirted one side of the gully. Several times the Cross-bearer fell, and each time Lucero offered to shoulder the burden, although from the start he found that he could not even heave it off the ground. By the time they reached the Hutchins' fences, the One in White was utterly spent. Then it was that an idea flashed through Lucero's mind.

"My Lord, You cannot go much farther this way," he said. "What You need is a horse."

A wondering look was the only answer.

"The man who lives here has a beautiful animal. Let me fetch it for You. I will bring it back tonight."

But those gentle eyes in the dark plainly said, "No."

"Do not fear, Lord; it will not throw You. It is a gentle-man's horse. It is an *alazán,* a sorrel worthy of You."

The thorn-crowned Head moved from side to side, but Lucero had already begun to climb the steep side of the arroyo. The corral was crowded with mustangs which did not seem to feel his presence. The doors of the shed gnashed their hinges and creaked loudly when he opened them, but the sleeping dogs nearby did not even cock an ear. There was a saddle astride the sorrel's stall, and this he slid over its back and deftly cinched. In a few minutes he was leading a very willing steed through the gates and down the arroyo; but to his great surprise he found his companions gone. The only signs of their having been there were the blood spots and the prints of feet and cross on the wet scurf. He noticed that they led away across the valley, and even thought that he had caught a glimpse of the lantern's light up on the mesa. As the horse began to stamp impatiently, Lucero clambered into the saddle, and the sorrel started off after sniffing at the spoor like a large hound on the hunt.

Most of the townsfolk were in church Good Friday morning when Tom Hutchins stormed about town rounding up a posse of vigilantes to track the horse-thief. Maldonado joined them, for he had gone to see his sick friend early that morning and found him missing. He alone had an inkling as to who the thief might be, and his fears grew apace the farther they rode along the hoof-tracks which ran out in a bee line past the mesa to a stretch of prairie country beyond. Well past midday, they spied a lone rider in the distance slowly approaching the little cluster of hovels that make up the village of La Jara. The posse spurred their mounts and in a short while closed in a prancing ring around the sweated and hoof-sore Hutchins' horse, the half-conscious Lucero clinging to its mane.

▼▼▼

La Jara gets its name from the only tree in that neighbor-
hood, a big willow in front of the small adobe chapel. One of
its branches makes a half-arch over the old mission cross, and
under this branch they drove a team and wagon, which they took
from one of the inhabitants for the business on hand. They put
Lucero on the wagon, dropped a lasso about his neck, and tied
the rope to the limb a few inches above his woolen cap. Slowly
the poor fellow began to realize what the men were about.
Blinking his galled and red eyes, he looked over his captors. In
addition to McBride, who stood beside him on the wagon box,
he could make out Goldfeld, Archevéque, Hutchins, Morelli,
Toribio Lopez and Maldonado — all in a threatening group,
except for his friend, who stood quietly apart to the left of the
big cross. To him Lucero stretched out his frozen hands.

"Maldonado, *amigo,* you are a politician and a lawyer. Tell
them that I am a dying man who has done no harm."

"I have done my best, Lucero, but they will not listen. They caught you with Hutchins' *alazán,* and that is enough for them. I always warned you, my friend, about stealing horses."

"But I did not steal this horse. I only borrowed it for my Lord Jesus Christ. He was so weak —"

"Say, what kind of an excuse is that?" Hutchins spoke up. "Boys, this ain't no sewing bee, it's a necktie party. He stole my sorrel, didn't he? String him up, then, the horse-thief!"

"Lord, remember me!" Lucero cried out hoarsely, turning to the mission cross. At once his bleared eyelids flipped with amazement, for there He was on that cross, He Whom Lucero had been tracking all night long. He was naked now and nailed to the cross, not merely tied. He looked like the crucifix back home in the church of San Ramon, only larger and bloodier.

"Lord, remember me," he pleaded.

Then he heard His Voice for the first time, soft and sweet and solemn: "My son, this day you will be with Me. . . ."

The bystanders were so fascinated by Lucero's strange be-havior that he thought that they too saw and heard the Lord.

"Lord, forgive these *caballeros*," he cried. "They think that I did steal that horse. And my good friend Maldonado —"

"Your friend Maldonado," said the Crucified, "is a robber of widows. He smothered the Señora Lopez and is not sorry."

Lucero's voice rose beseechingly. "But, Lord Jesus, Maldonado is sorry that he killed old Doña Encarnación!"

Like a flash Toribio Lopez stepped forward with drawn pistol and with a curse fired at Maldonado. At the same instant, the branch overhead shuddered as the team of horses, startled by the report, jerked the wagon away and left Lucero dangling beneath the willow. The horsemen quietly stole away, and the three-o'clock sun came out from behind a cloud and shone down on the bare mission cross, on a man lying face downward at the left, and another hanging from a tree at the right.

III

HUNCHBACK MADONNA

▼▼▼

HUNCHBACK MADONNA

LD and crumbling, the squat-built adobe mission of El Tordo sits in a hollow high up near the snow-capped Truchas. A few clay houses huddle close to it like tawny chicks about a ruffled old hen. On one of the steep slopes, which has the peaks for a background, sleeps the ancient graveyard with all its inhabitants, or what little is left of them. The town itself is quite as lifeless during the winter months, when the few folks that live there move down to warmer levels by the Rio Grande; but when the snows have gone, except for the white crusts on the peaks, they return to herd their sheep and goats, and with them comes a stream of pious pilgrims and curious sightseers which lasts throughout the spring and summer weather.

They come to see and pray before the stoop-shouldered Virgin, people from as far south as Belen who from some accident or some spinal or heart affliction are shoulder-bent and want to walk straight again. Others, whose faith is not so simple or who have no faith at all, have come from many parts of the country and asked the way to El Tordo, not only to see the curiously painted Madonna in which the natives put so much stock, but to visit a single grave in a corner of the *campo santo* which, they have heard, is covered in spring with a profusion of wild flowers, whereas the other sunken ones are bare altogether, or at the most sprinkled only with sagebrush and tumbleweed. And, of course, they want to hear from the lips of some old inhabitant the history of the town and the church, the painting and the grave, and particularly of Mana Seda.

No one knows, or cares to know, when the village was born. It is more thrilling to say, with the natives, that the first settlers came up from the Santa Clara valley long before the railroad came to New Mexico, when the Indians of Nambé and Taos still used bows and arrows and obsidian clubs; when it took a week to go to Santa Fé, which looked no different from the other northern towns at the time, only somewhat bigger. After the men had allotted the scant farming land among themselves, and each family raised its adobe hut of one or two rooms to begin with, they set to making adobes for a church that would shoulder above their homes as a guardian parent. On a high, untillable slope they marked out as their God's acre a plot which was to be surrounded by an adobe wall. It was not long before large pines from the forest nearby had been carved into beams and corbels and hoisted into their places on the thick walls. The women themselves mud-plastered the tall walls outside with their bare hands; within they made them a soft white with a lime mixture applied with the woolly side of sheepskins.

The Padre, whose name the people do not remember, was so pleased with the building, and with the crudely wrought reredos behind the altar, that he promised to get at his own ex- pense a large hand-painted *Nuestra Señora de Guadalupe* to hang in the middle of the *retablo*. But this had to wait until the next traders' ox-drawn caravan left Santa Fé for Chihuahua in

Old Mexico and came back again. It would take years, perhaps, if there was no such painting ready and it must be made to order.

With these first settlers of El Tordo had come an old woman who had no relatives in the place they had left. For no apparent reason she had chosen to cast her lot with the emigrants, and they had willingly brought her along in one of their wooden-wheeled *carretas,* had even built her a room in the protective shadow of the new church. For that had been her work before, sweeping the house of God, ringing the Angelus morning, noon and night, adorning the altar with lace cloths and flowers, when there were flowers. She even persuaded the Padre, when the first May came around, to start an ancient custom prevalent in her place of origin: that of having little girls dressed as queens and their maids-in-waiting present bunches of flowers to the Virgin Mary every evening in May. She could not wait for the day when the Guadalupe picture would arrive.

They called her *Mana Seda,* "Sister Silk." Nobody knew why; they had known her by no other name. The women thought

she had got it long ago for being always so neat, or maybe because she embroidered so many altar-cloths. But the men said it
was because she looked so much like a silk-spinning spider; for
she was very much humpbacked — so bent forward that she could
look up only sideways and with effort. She always wore black,
a black shiny dress and black shawl with long leg-like fringes
and, despite her age and deformity, she walked about quite
swiftly and noiselessly. "Yes," they said, "like the black widow
spider."

Being the cause of the May devotions at El Tordo, she took
it upon herself to provide the happy girls with flowers for the
purpose. The geraniums which she grew in her window were
used up the first day, as also those that other women had tended
in their own homes. So she scoured the slopes around the village
for wild daisies and Indian paintbrush, usually returning in the
late afternoon with a shawlful to spill at the eager children's
feet. Toward the end of May she had to push deeper into the
forest, whence she came back with her tireless, short-stepped

spider-run, her arms and shawl laden with wild iris and cosmos, verbenas and mariposa lilies from the pine shadows.

This she did year after year, even after the little "queens" of former Mays got married and new tots grew up to wear their veils. Mana Seda's one regret was that the image of the Virgin of Guadalupe had not come, had been lost on the way when the Comanches or Apaches attacked and destroyed the Chihuahua-Santa Fé ox-train.

One year in May (it was two days before the close of the month), when the people were already whispering among themselves that Mana Seda was so old she must die soon, or else last forever, she was seen hurrying into the forest early in the morning, to avail herself of all the daylight possible, for she had to go far into the wooded canyons this time. At the closing services of May there was to be, not one queen, but a number of them with their attendants. Many more flowers were needed for this, and the year had been a bad one for flowers, since little snow had fallen the winter before.

Mana Seda found few blooms in her old haunts, here and there an aster with half of its petals missing or drought-toasted, or a faded columbine fast wilting in the cool but moistureless shade. But she must find enough flowers; otherwise the good heavenly Mother would have a sad and colorless farewell this May. On and on she shuttled in between the trunks of spruce and fir, which grew thicker and taller and closer-set as the canyon grew narrower. Further up she heard the sound of trickling water; surely the purple iris and freckled lily flames would be rioting there, fresh and without number. She was not disappointed, and without pausing to recover her breath, began lustily to snap off the long, luscious stems and lay them on her shawl, spread out on the little meadow. Her haste was prompted by the darkness closing in through the evergreens, now turning blacker and blacker, not with approaching dusk, but with the smoky pall of thunderheads that had swallowed up the patches of blue among the tops of the forest giants.

Far away arose rumblings that grew swiftly louder and nearer. The great trees, which always whispered to her even on quiet, sunny days, began to hiss and whine angrily at the unseen wind that swayed them and swung their arms like maidens unwilling to be kissed or danced with. And then a deafening sound exploded nearby with a blinding bluish light. Others followed, now on the right or on the left, now before or behind, as Mana Seda, who had thrown her flower-weighted mantle on her arched back, started to run — in which direction she knew not, for the rain was slashing down in sheets that blurred the dark boles and boulders all around her.

At last she fell, whimpering prayers to the holy Virgin with a water-filled mouth that choked her. Of a sudden, sunlight began to fall instead between the towering trees, now quiet and dripping with emeralds and sapphires. The storm had passed by, the way spring rains in the Truchas Mountains do, as suddenly as it had come. In a clearing not far ahead, Mana Seda saw a little adobe hut. On its one chimney stood a wisp of smoke,

like a white feather. Still clutching her heavy, rain-soaked shawl,
she ran to it and knocked at the door, which was opened by an
astonished young man with a short, sharp knife in his hand.

▼▼▼

"I thought the mountain's bowels where the springs come
from had burst," she was telling the youth, who meanwhile
stirred a pot of brown beans that hung with a pail of coffee
over the flames in the corner fireplace. "But our most holy Lady
saved me when I prayed to her, *gracias a Dios.* The lightning
and the water stopped, and I saw her flying above me. She had
a piece of sky for a veil, and her skirt was like the beautiful red
roses at her feet. She showed me your house."

Her host tried to hide his amusement by taking up his work
again, a head he had been carving on the end of a small log.
She saw that he was no different from the grown boys of El
Tordo, dark and somewhat lean-bodied in his plain homespun.
All about, against the wall and in niches, could be seen several

other images, wooden and gaily colored *bultos,* and more *santos* painted on pieces of wood or hide. Mana Seda guessed that this must be the young stranger's trade, and grew more confident because of it. As she spread out her shawl to dry before the open fire, her load of flowers rolled out soggily on the bare earth floor. Catching his questioning stare, she told him what they were for, and about the church and the people of El Tordo.

"But that makes me think of the apparition of Our Lady of Guadalupe," he said. "Remember how the Indian Juan Diego filled his blanket with roses, as Mary most holy told him to do? And how, when he let down his *tilma* before the Bishop, out fell the roses, and on it was the miraculous picture of the Mother of God?"

Yes, she knew the story well; and she told him about the painting of the Guadalupe which the priest of El Tordo had ordered brought from Mexico and which was lost on the way. Perhaps, if the Padre knew of this young man's ability, he would pay him for making one. Did he ever do work for churches? And what was his name?

"My name is Esquipula," he replied. *"Sí,* I have done work for the Church. I made the *retablo* of 'San Francisco' for his church in Ranchos de Taos, and also the 'Cristo' for Santa Cruz. The 'Guadalupe' at San Juan, I painted it. I will gladly paint another for your chapel." He stopped all of a sudden, shut his eyes tight, and then quickly leaned toward the bent old figure who was helping herself to some coffee. "Why do you not let me paint one right now — on your shawl!"

She could not answer at first. Such a thing was unheard of. Besides, she had no other *tápalo* to wear. And what would the people back home say when she returned wearing the Virgin on her back? What would She say?

"You can wear the picture turned inside where nobody can see it. Look! You will always have holy Mary with you, hovering over you, hugging your shoulders and your breast! Come," he continued, seeing her ready to yield, "it is too late for you to go back to El Tordo. I will paint it now, and tomorrow I and Mariquita will take you home."

"And who is Mariquita?" she wanted to know.

"Mariquita is my little donkey," was the reply.

Mana Seda's black shawl was duly hung and spread tight against a bare stretch of wall, and Esquipula lost no time in tracing with white chalk the outlines of the small wood-print which he held in his left hand as a model. The actual laying of the colors, however, went much slower because of the shawl's rough and unsized texture. Darkness came, and Esquipula lit an oil lamp, which he held in one hand as he applied the pigments with the other. He even declined joining his aged guest at her evening meal of beans and stale *tortillas,* because he was not hungry, he explained, and the picture must be done.

Once in a while the painter would turn from his work to look at Mana Seda, who had become quite talkative, something the people back at El Tordo would have marveled at greatly. She was recounting experiences of her girlhood which, she explained, were more vivid than many things that had happened recently.

Only once did he interrupt her, and that without thinking first. He said, almost too bluntly: "How did you become hunch-backed?"

Mana Seda hesitated, but did not seem to take the question amiss. Patting her shoulder as far as she could reach to her bulging back, she answered: "The woman who was nursing me dropped me on the hard dirt floor when I was a baby, and I grew up like a ball. But I do not remember, of course. My being bent out of shape did not hurt me until the time when other little girls of my age were chosen to be flower-maids in May. When I was older, and other big girls rejoiced at being chosen May queens, I was filled with bitter envy. God forgive me, I even cursed. I at last made up my mind never to go to the May devotions, nor to Mass either. In the place of my birth, the shores of the Rio Grande are made up of wet sand which sucks in every living creature that goes in; I would go there and return no more. But something inside told me the Lord would be most pleased if I helped the other lucky girls with their flowers. That would make me a flower-bearer every day. Esquipula, my son, I have been doing this for seventy-four Mays!"

Mana Seda stopped and reflected in deep silence. The youth who had been painting absent-mindedly and looking at her, now noticed for the first time that he had made the Virgin's shoulders rather stooped, like Mana Seda's, though not quite so much. His first impulse was to run the yellow sun-rays into them and cover up the mistake, but for no reason he decided to let things stand as they were. By and by he put the last touches to his *oeuvre de caprice,* offered the old lady his narrow cot in a corner, and went out to pass the night in Mariquita's humble shed.

The following morning saw a young man leading a grey burro through the forest, and on the patient animal's back swayed a round black shape, grasping her mantle with one hand while the other held tight to the small wooden saddle. Behind her, their bright heads bobbing from its wide mouth, rode a sack full of iris and tiger-lilies from the meadow where the storm had caught Mana Seda the day before. Every once in a while, Esquipula had to stop the beast and go after some new flower which the rider had spied from her perch; sometimes she made him climb up a steep rock for a crannied blossom he would have passed unnoticed.

The sun was going down when they at last trudged into El Tordo and halted before the church, where the priest stood surrounded by a bevy of inquiring, disappointed girls. He rushed forth immediately to help Mana Seda off the donkey, while the children pounced upon the flowers with shouts of glee. Asking questions and not waiting for answers, he led the stranger and his still stranger charge into his house, meanwhile giving orders that the burro be taken to his barn and fed.

Mana Seda dared not sit with the Padre at table and hied herself to the kitchen for her supper. Young Esquipula, however, felt very much at ease, answering all his host's questions intelligently, at which the pastor was agreeably surprised, but not quite so astonished as when he heard for the first time of Mana Seda's childhood disappointments.

"Young man," he said, hurriedly finishing his meal, "there is little time to lose. Tonight is the closing of May — and it will be done, although we are unworthy." Dragging his chair closer to the youth, he plotted out his plan in excited whispers which fired Esquipula with an equal enthusiasm.

▼▼▼

The last bell was calling the folk of El Tordo in the cool of the evening. Six queens with their many white-veiled maids stood in a nervous, noisy line at the church door, a garden of flowers in their arms. The priest and the stranger stood on guard facing them, begging them to be quiet, looking anxiously at the people who streamed past them into the edifice. Mana Seda finally appeared and tried to slide quietly by, but the Padre barred her way and pressed a big basket filled with flowers and

lighted candles into her brown, dry hands. At the same time
Esquipula took off her black shawl and dropped over her grey
head and hunched form a precious veil of Spanish lace.

In her amazement she could not protest, could not even
move a step, until the Padre urged her on, whispering into her
ear that it was the holy Virgin's express wish. And so Mana
Seda led all the queens that evening, slowly and smoothly, not
like a black widow now, folks observed, but like one of those
little white moths moving over alfalfa fields in the moonlight.
It was the happiest moment of her long life. She felt that she
must die from pure joy, and many others observing her, thought
so too.

She did not die then; for some years afterward, she
wore the new black *tápalo* the Padre gave her in exchange for
the old one, which Esquipula installed in the *retablo* above the
altar. But toward the last she could not gather any more flowers
on the slopes, much less in the forest. They buried her in a corner of the *campo santo,* and the following May disks of daisies

and bunches of verbenas came up on her grave. It is said they have been doing it ever since, for curious travelers to ask about, while pious pilgrims come to pray before the hunchback Madonna.

CPSIA information can be obtained at www.ICGtesting.com
Printed in the USA
LVOW13s0130130614

389822LV00001B/25/P